Table of contents

Chapter 1

She is…

A burning sun.

The fine print:

I have depression.

I have anxiety.

I have borderline multi-personality disorder. I think it is pretty freaking awesome.

I have had suicidal thoughts.

I have cut myself with a bade more than 17 times last time I counted.

I still have some scars to show for it.

My poems are full of imagery, so I am sorry in advance if you feel like you are there during some of my episodes.

Final warning: I am still here, ready to set fire to all things evil. Why? Well, continue reading to find out babes.

Sunflower

March 14, 2017

It all started with a seed
sprouting from all the pain
I would bleed from my past
that is so dark
like the core of a sunflower.

I needed appreciation
without the greed of saying
I made you.

Love broke me.
It knew that I was fertile like soil,
but it was not cautious with me.

You see the image of your past lover.

Your imagination with hesitation

shows you an empty field

with your lover in sight.

The sun's shinning bright,

as you run to your lover,

within an instant it goes from day to
night.

And the once empty field

fills with soaring sunflowers

just to take your eyes off of her.

Your lover disappears, and your fears show

your adrenaline increases as you see her
go.

You start breathing heavily in the dark
sunflower field

lit by nothing but the moon.

You feel lonely, but you are not alone.
Your love was lost. Your lover's gone.

Justice

Senses

April 13, 2017

I seek validation in your touch,
the way you hug me, kiss me,

"so, called" make love to me.
You've neglected me.

I just wish you could see,
how broken I am like shattered glass,
that shattered wholly images of your past.
You knew this would eventually clash
and burn.

Fear is something I would smell,
like a dog sensing fear in a human.
I took a chance at loving you.
You feared loving me.

I'd kiss your lips and taste
the bitterness of your secret
Fruits are supposed to be sweet,
our love was bitter sweet.

I hope that you hear
my voice every time you question
whether or not you had a choice
in staying or leaving.
You made me leave you.

Running

April 13, 2017

I am searching for a love
that I will never find.
It's a search that keeps me running.
I am chasing a love
that is greater than any ordinary love.

I am confidently lost,
Just to discover someone
who is lost in the same way
that I am.

I am worthy of love,
But only if it is pure.

When we find each other
we will be finished chasing
the love we have been running after.

A Father's Love
September 20, 2017

It started with you
I was your job, but you failed me.
I was supposed to look towards you
to determine the guy, I should marry.

Tough love is an excuse
to cover up verbal abuse.
Where did your love go?

It went to my heart,
but the love you gave just tore me apart.

You went wrong when you sent it my way
The love you gave will never stay.

It turned into pain,
so, in my mind, pain was all that remained.

Eyes

September 27, 2017

Hurt. Abuse. Tragedy.

Created such beauty in your eyes.

Your reflection hides your pain.

You create a positive out of a negative.

You're a walking mask.

Smiles on your face

replace your frowns.

Laughs heard in the night

substitute your cries.

You hide from the world.

Honesty. Loyalty. Curiosity.

unlocks the real you.

I hold the key you've been hiding.

I'm beside you when you're fighting.

I see your eyes,

green without envy.

Green like the grass

that is greener on the other side.

I will forever be right by your side.

Love> Youth

September 29, 2017

Young.

I am 18.

You are 20.

Dumb.

I dare to disagree.

I love you and you love me.

Broke.

Well most young adults start off this way,

long as we are working towards stability,

I will forever have you and you will
forever have me.

Roles

September 29, 2017

I played a fool for this so-called love.
Both eyes were on you and nobody was above.

I gave up myself

to have a place in your heart

and as my lover

you couldn't even play your part.

Queen

September 29, 2017

I do not think you ever feared losing me,

because if you did you would have treated
me like royalty.

You would have proved your loyalty,

but instead you chose to practice pre-
adultery.

Queens should never be competing with
peasants,

the thought of you, just became so
unpleasant.

She could never take my thrown,

and fulfill it without lacking.

She could never wear my crown,
Her bags, she is unpacking.

She could never have my king,
she's not worth the wedding ring.

She could never run my palace,
She is lost like Alice.

She is not only a peasant,
she is the person taking you away from your
blessing.

Thank You

September 29, 2017

Broken.

I was before I met you,

but since I met you, I knew that I would
never forget you.

Before you, I didn't believe that a girl
like me deserved love

or that this thing called love would ever
settle for me.

I always felt like I was never enough,

especially when I was weak, and life was
getting rough.

You changed that for me.

You were always there for me.

Therefore, I thank you.

Unconditionally.

Smoke Session

September 29,2017

So, I have never smoked before.

Apparently, that was a given statement.

I found myself lost and beneath everyone
like a basement.

I am sitting there while mother earth was
in rotation,

Thinking about this dude in which I had
relations.

I came in only because they boys were hot
boxing in the pantry.

Didn't realize that this would make me feel
good and dandy.

I didn't plan on smoking I just fell in
love with the contact.

It's like I was divorcing all of my issues
like signing the dotted like on a contract.

He gets the blunt and passes it to me.

I was like no I can't do, I can't even see.

It's dark as fuck, no light but the tip of
the blunt.

I was chilling, but I wasn't even trying to
front.

Peer pressure was not the issue here

It was either hit the blunt

or grab the nearest tissue for my tears.

I was tired of crying,

so, I hit the blunt

and instantly started dying.

Previously he said to me,

"Hit the blunt, you don't want to waste
it."

I was like "nah man you would mess up the
rotation."

He was like "girl if you waste this blunt,
then it will burn to ashes."

I hit the blunt like a virgin

And it hit my chest like a heart attack.

Zac

The Wait

December 15, 2017

I've been waiting on something to happen

a lightning strike from above

a white light with singing white doves

I've been waiting on a sign

I've been waiting on the pieces to the
puzzle

to unravel and then ravel back together
again

I've been waiting on my chance to win

I've been trying to move in silence

yet everyone still seems to notice my
motions.

They watch my every move,

And laugh when I lose focus.

I've been staying up until the early
mornings,

sleep is too close to death,

no loved one's mourning

seems like I'm the only one

mourning my life, before death
I've been waiting on my life to turn around
before I am no longer breathing
I am six feet above ground,

yet looks can be deceiving.

Stalker Alert

December 15, 2017

Every time I do something in my life

this cold-hearted person runs to tell my
dad.

This makes me furious, angry, and downright
mad.

It could be a friend or foe,

a family member or a hoe

(yes, a tool, she's being used somehow,
right?).

I thought that blood was supposed to be
tight.

Rather it's the truth or a lie,

they take it and run.

How deep could that love run?

Seems like they are just running my life
down the drain,

this bullshit is taking over my brain

literally.

I obsess over this person as they obsess
over me.

Why mess with an unstable girl

mentally?

Is it because I found love

and you never will?

Is it the college degree I'm working on

and the future money I will be making.

Maybe it is my beauty seen to cover the
pain,

maybe a letter covered in blood would
explain my reasoning?

Or maybe the murder I wrote was not enough
for you?

it should have been your murderous hands
that set me free,

but with a heart like yours, you showed no
mercy.

Hazel Eyes and Goodbyes

February 8, 2018

My eyes catch your hazel eyes

As you bump my shoulder passing me in the
hallway.

I couldn't hear your "excuse me" over the
noisy students

The hallway's laughter cautioned me

like the wet floor sign

Under me as my tears fall to the floor.

I dry up my salt water eyes,

But my eyes are still sun flamed red.

Last week, you called it off, unfortunately

Instead of my lover, you are now my bully.

My eyelids cover my heart from your
devilish eyes.

When we glance-

then we look away startled towards the end,

I'll snuggle with your shirt that you let
me borrow.

When I hear your voice, I cannot forget

The last time your hands caressed my skin.

Your eyes gleaming throughout the night.

Your fingertips soothing my tense limbs,

As they dangle from my torso, numb.

There is no way I'd forget your presence-

Which I would consider diminished,

non-existent, and ghost-like

I should have looked through

The bull to see the manure,

but I focused on the pupils in your eyes.

Honesty

February 8, 2018

If by honest you mean as honest as a parent
lying

To their child about the tooth fairy, the
dryness of the dirt in the dessert,

The surprise of a knife in your dishwater-

Then Yes, every last poem is valid, every
heartbreak,

healed, and damaged. Pause. I have created
them-all of them-

And when I say I am engaged, it means I
engaged

all of them, an entire cult of past con-
men.

Could you imagine the inconsistency, the
lies, the betrayal?

Currently, my fiancés have to build a home

for us-with one building the foundation,
one pouring the cement

Into the layout. One focusing on the
plumbing, and one works on the roofing.

One pays the bills, while another will mow
the lawn while

Another reads the newspaper and smokes a
cigar. And each

one of them are waiting for a call back.

Purging

February 8, 2018

This smoke session didn't go so well,

there is no telling how many stories I had
to tell.

One was about this boy who claimed he loved
me,

yet he didn't because I was never his one
or his only.

He had a girl, yet he was still searching

It's like the day after a purge, but he was
still purging.

He filled my head up with lies.

I was so drunk and high that night, I might
have even cried.

Everyone was there, but they didn't have my
back.

It seemed like I was sitting there waiting
on Love to attack.

Seems like love was defeated by hate,

I wonder how many of you all can relate?

I made a fool out of myself that night

I apologized for it, but this just didn't
feel right.

He said, "You fall for people to easily."

In reality, I fell for the people who
were misleading.

I was the person who was misled,

as you were leading me to your bed

reality pounding at my head

whole body numb as if I were dead.

Feels

February 13, 2018

I feel like crying.

I feel like dying.

I feel like giving up and no longer trying.

Silence

March 9, 2018

Razor blades and grenades

My eyes view the world in fifty shades

-of red.

I wish you were dead,

Oh, wait that mission is complete.

I hated to be alive and being the victim

-of defeat.

I was concrete and my feet

Were planted on the ground,

Yet I was running out

-of time.

Most people were given lemons, I was given
a lime

I couldn't make lemonade. There was no
first aid.

I slit my wrist with no assistant

-of mine.

How are you? I am fine.

That's the line I tell them every time.

The room was quiet for once, free

-of tears.

I removed the burden that was there for a
number of years.

I am a bird, now I can fly.

I always wanted to see my face as I die

-of silence.

Coma

March 9, 2018

If I was in a deep sleep with nothing

but memories on repeat,

how would I remember you?

Would I remember your crooked smile,

your curly hair,

your green eyes?

Would I remember your soothing voice,

your tickled fingertips,

your inner thighs?

How about the way you held me close

when I needed you the most?

What about the way you entered my body

just to find your way to my heart?

If I woke up right now,

would you be there to welcome me?

Or would you leave my side to

be a part of the rest of humanity?

Patches

March 9, 2018

I don't want to waste my time.
I am a dime and my love so divine.

We need closure
to the exposure.

Heal my wounds with stitches
my scars will only be a few inches.

You filled my cup,
So, I'm your problem to heal.
You have to patch me up
by giving me something new to reveal.

In Heat

March 10, 2018

I remember the night I cried
because an old friend called me with some
news.
She had unprotected sex and discovered a
bruise
or few, she had way too much pride

in her inner thighs to protect
herself from his infectious loving.
She was weakened by his hood ways,
his illegal gun, his tattoos, and his third
leg

she was just trying to live,
but he harmed her.
he didn't know he had a gift to give
he just wanted to keep her warmer

on the winter nights
filled with snow and frost bite.

In

March 11, 2018

The situation I am in
Is boiling like the heat from hell.
I cannot win

Then again,
I simply cannot tell.
I was sitting in the den

With a bunch of men
Who wanted to wish me well.
I started to grin

Before the sin,
That was an epic fail.
I touched his chin

And remembered when
This fling was going swell,
He caressed my skin

Said breathe out then in
I am waiting to exhale.

He reaches in to fix what is within,
But the line between love and hate is thin.

Home

March 12, 2018

I am searching for something.

A love. A connection. A bond.

I am searching for a place

That I can feel safe.

I've searched for it

In a house that belonged to my mom,

A house in the country owned by my father,

an apartment full of niggas and weed and
shit,

Fuckboys back to back trying to get over on
me,

A stressed mother trying to find a home of
her own,

a retired tough love giving father,

A forbidden relationship with the same sex,

an apartment across a bridge with a guy who
has a hold on me,

my own place where I can't even feel safe,

my apartment with a pothead

who is no longer in the army an alcoholic

asking me for urine to pass a drug test
roommate who threatens me,

*take a deep mental breath, I am still
searching.

a lover who let me have my way with a guy
who claimed he loved me,

a psychologist who keeps telling me I'm not
crazy,

a best friend who agrees with my self-
diagnosis of depression and anxiety and bi-
polar disorder,

a lover who calls me a bitch accidentally
on purpose,

an envious sister who snitched and made up
stories about me

just because I wouldn't pick her kids up
from school,

a niece who is trying to find attention by
lifting her shirt up on her dance videos,

a message from my dad about Lexi
Washington,

a search for this Lexi Washington,

a lie to make me feel better even though it
made me feel worse,

and a subject that's subject to change.

Can you change me?

Alter my mood swings,

take away my depression and obsession with
you.

I need happiness. I just do not know how to
obtain it.

I beg you to take me away from this home

that has me buried under it like a burden.

I have to be free. I have to discover me.

This job is like finding a grain of salt

Dissolved in the deep blue sea.

Topless

March 12, 2018

I was asked to take my shirt off
for a photoshoot that wasn't even my own.
I was eighteen years old and a rebel
So, I felt like I was kind of grown.

I wanted to feel pretty.
I wanted to feel admired.
In reality, my body was
Pretty drained and tired.

I took off my shirt
Enough to not have it in sight of the
camera,
then he asked for her to grab the baby oil
I am no baby.

I was glistening afterwards like the sea.
I'm pretty sure that man looked right
through me.

Let me know

March 13, 2018

Without a call or a text,
I feel lonely and disconnected
from the people
who I thought loved me.

I always have to text first,
Just to beg for
Another human's attention
Another human's loving

That they barely have to give
Let alone take mine
And pocket that empty loving
Shared between the disconnected.

I have a habit of
Texting people 3 words
"I love you"
So, I can hear it back
And feel it too.

I just want to feel something
Even if it's not the best for me.
I just want to feel a sense of unity.

Dirt

March 13,2018

Just like a dead flower

I lack the

Water

Sunlight

And nutrients

To survive.

Teenagers in love
with their hormones
taking over their aching bones.

They are hypnotized
by their sexual desires
creating unwanted fires.

They cannot put them out,
she will live the teenage dream
meddling with his forbidden love schemes.

She would disobey and rebel
against her loving mother
just to be with her forsaken lover.

She will let her windows down
in the backseat of her car
just for a quick penetration to travel far.

Far as in take me pass the clouds
so that we can live forever
leave you I will never.

Our summer nights,
I would not trade them for anything
even though we are not together.

Solo

June 13,2018

As long as I am here

I know that you will

always be near me

If I call you will reply

if I fall you will deny

that you were the one to push me

I overdosed on your lies

As you whispered dark secrets

in between my thighs

as you drowned my tears

with something in a red solo cup.

Hear no Evil

June 17, 2018

The night sky is as dark as the moon will
allow,

covered by the stormy clouds that tend to
wonder how,

we can take all the rain it drops on our
shoulders

knocking us down like big, baffling
boulders.

We stand tall with our chest against the
winds

working on the problems we have embedded
within

trying to silence the evil we hear,

searching for God who is always near.

I close my eyes to see the face of the
devil,

I scream and yell and pick up the shovel

to bury my demons deep inside

a place where fears run to hide.

We are awakened from sleep

"I pray the lord my soul to keep"

We were in for a trick not treat

before we were damned to our defeat.

No feeling

July 2,2018

I feel nothing in your kisses

I feel nothing in your strokes,

Yet they say I have feelings for you.

I feel anxious when you speak

I feel love at your defeat

Yet they say I'm in love with someone new.

I feel nothing when you touch me

I feel nothing when you fuck me

Yet my body is numb to this.

I feel butterflies hearing your name

I feel at times I am insane

Yet I am blind in this abyss.

Chapter 2

She is...

The only one.

Sorry in Advance

August 19,2018

I run away from things that could make me
smile.

I settle for people who won't go the extra
mile.

I want more than what I give to another

I'm in need of love not another lover.

I struggle with depression and anxiety

but I blame my ex for that shit.

I was a flower that would grow next to
what's hit.

I am a variety...

-of different women that you're not used
to.

I look for chill vibes and good energy if
I'm with you.

A vibe so strong could scare me away,

but I promise I'll be good at the end of
the day.

I've got some baggage from when I used to
have fun

listening to drake thinking

look what you've done

I used to cry but now I choose not to,

I will be me, with or without you.

Backseat

August 22, 2018

No intent to get closure

I wanted reassurance

I wanted to use you

No need for a title

No need to talk

I wanted you silent

I wanted you inside it

No need to fear

I don't want your time

No need to text back

No need to love me

I don't want you

I want you in the backseat

No need to arrest me

No need to undress me

I'm just here for the ride

Oxymoron

August 25,2018

Damsel and distress
In search of an actual hero
My life became a mess
But now I'm down to zero

You caught me in a phase
Where others took advantage
Your feelings were like a maze
So, hell is where I managed

You were a beautiful nightmare
Until the lights went out
You were a blessing and a curse
Water during a drought

Damsel in distress
Forced to save the day
I knew happiness would come
Once the dragon went away.

Bruises

August 26, 2018

You left your bed

You left the image in my head

But you didn't have to leave these bruises

You used me

And abused me

But you didn't have to be so useless.

You fucked up

Another will luck up

But now you're acting clueless.

You said let it flow

I said let it go

But you wanted to keep me hostage.

You wanted to complicate the situation

I wanted more than your participation

But you wanted to be an asshole.

You couldn't get your shit together

I had to pick up the pieces

I could have left you for plenty of reasons

I faked my happiness for your sanity

I did more than what you asked of me

I was too damn nice.

I don't regret a thing

Wish you kept the ring

I don't need another reminder

Of another failed relationship.

Dog Trainer

September 6, 2018

I have loved way too many times to count

I loved a boy, a man, a woman

and now you want my love?

Do I have enough love inside to be giving?

or should I be selfish like the others
were?

Should I let myself love you?

I loved when I received disappointment

I continued to expect a different result
out of the same guy.

I should have put that same love into
myself.

Maybe I would not be depressed

or pressed by these other bitches

They are bitches right?

They tolerate disrespect from these boys

They have no respect for themselves

and they will let any dog in no matter the
breed.

Maybe I should have loved my dog more,

she sat on my lap and gave me kisses

why was her puppy love not enough compared
to these dogs?

I mean... when a dog sees a bone, he will
chase it right?

nobody ever chased me

Not a dog, a teenage boy, a Fuckboy, a man,
nor a woman.

Am I not worth the run?

The chase on a summer night for a summer
fling?

how about a wife to be, where is my ring?

I am worth more than what they valued me.

I am worth more than a DM and a whistle as
I pass by

I am worth your honesty and compassion.

I am worth the love I give that is AGAPE

I am worth your time and your money.

I need some dedication and appreciation.

I had to train these dogs

just so the next bitch can be buried under
a pile of dirt

At least they chased the bone, right?

Right, but after they came right back to me

a loyal dog comes back to its owner.

I have a whole animal shelter outside my
door.

Impatient

September 6, 2018

It seems like I am rushing this, but I am
not

I am just afraid to never obtain greatness

I want to find my future husband now so
that we can grow

I do not want to be lonely when I am old
and grey

I want to have my life in order now

I refuse to be a failure like the people I
just so happen to be surrounded by

I have a plan now that could help me reach
my full potential

I must be successful, but I still need
support and guidance

It seems like I am anxious because I am

I am good to those who hurt me repeatedly.
I must be a damn fool.

I push away someone who may actually love
me (out of fear)

I pretend to be strong just to go home and
cry behind closed doors

I am a fucking wreck, but I must not be labeled weak in anyone's book other than my father's

He has made me cry more than a past lover. He showed me that crying is a weakness,

Call me impatient, irrational, or greedy.

I will disagree. I just know I do not want the life you live. It is depressing.

I want more out of life than what they teach you in school.

I want to travel the world and be free.

I want to heal the earth and its people.

I will push my poetry, model and get my degree.

I will be unstoppable. I will never be average or normal.

I am only 19, (20 now) yes, I know. but by the time I am well off into my life...

You will just be getting started with your own.

Dinner

September 6, 2018

We would sit there in silence

at the dinner table where we used to smile
and laugh.

We would pretend to be okay

we were not doing anything but hurting each
other.

We used to kiss and hug,

we do not show affection like we used to.

We used to love making dinner together.

we can't even have a meal without fighting.

I started to hate the way you would breathe

it would annoy the hell out of me.

I used to hate your voice,

I still do. that's why we text instead to
talk.

I used to love dinner time.

I used to love you.

I fucking hate you.

Disappointment

September 6,2018

I am used to it.

You aren't attracted to me sexually
That's not something that I am used to
I've been able to do a lot more to others
So, don't let this issue confuse you

I lack the experience you have
I'd rather take the pleasure than pain
but I'd take it for you
long as your energy remains the same

I don't want to become a problem
I want to make them go away
I will be under your command
And do whatever you say

I've been craved by both women and men

Dreamed of by boys

Making them grin

and put down their toys

I've been sexually frustrated

just like you

Only one man could please me

But he broke my heart in two

I decided to give it away

To another guy who was a stray

But it was too good to make him stay

He came too quick, dead giveaway.

I figured a girl would feel my pain

I got with her and my opinion remains the same

my body needs tender love and care

Not just anybody in my underwear

I surrendered to this one guy
Who begged me to give it to him
I had to reach cloud nine to do it
but before I could he released fluid.

I am lost, and I am confused
I've never had this problem with other
dudes
I had this girl tell me she could take it
I could too, just to fake it

I must admit it's too much for me
Or is it our lack of chemistry
I know you're into me, When you're into me
But could this love thing last until
infinity?

Insecure

September 28, 2018

I love my skin,

Even though it is pale and lacking melanin.

I love my freckles,

But I wish they were not covered in
breakouts.

I love my lips,

But they aren't as full as my soul sisters.

I love my hips,

But they aren't in the shape of an hour
glass.

I love my smile,

but sometimes it seems a little crooked.

I love my stomach,

Even though it is not like a belly dancer.

I love my pearl,

So much that I value it more than this
generation.

I love my glutes,

Even with my stretch marks and jiggles.

I love my mind,

Even though I have depression and anxiety.

I love my heart,

but sometimes it is way too big for me.

I love the skin I am in,

yet I forgot to mention my insecurities.

I Appreciate You

September 18, 2018

You'd call and check on me.

give me an abundance of hugs and kisses.

spend the night so I can sleep right.

be patient with me.

care and it shows.

stand your ground.

respect me.

do what you can.

always try to make me smile.

do anything to make me laugh.

kiss the pain away if you could.

I appreciate you and everything you'd do
good.

Enough

September 18,2018

I hope I am enough for you
When the water runs dry
When the money is spent
And after my heart is all bent.
I hope I am enough for you
After the late-night disagreements
And our over- under achievements
And our downfalls.
I hope I am enough for you
When I can't attract you in the way you
attract me
After the birth of a baby
And after I transition into the woman I am
supposed to be.
I am enough.
I just wonder if you're enough to handle
me.
When I can't cure my depression or my
anxiety
When I cry for no reason
When I have a bad day.
I hope I don't become too much

When my mood swings

And I hold all my anger in just to release
it on you

Or when I have a mental breakdown over
something I can't control.

We never know the plan.

I'm in long as you are.

If not just let me know.

Save Yourself

September 19, 2018

Your mind is being peeled back a few layers

To something that we must take control of:

Depression, anxiety, suicide, self-harm,

It's the devil's surprise.

He cannot win.

He will pick your brain

Again, and again

but you cannot give in.

He will creep up on your happiest days

To cover your sunshine with rain

He will provide the pain

But to him a cure is nonexistent

He will fool you within an instant

Flash of empty promises and an easy way out

His ways will never heal your heart

He will take away your ☼life that's worth
living.

You are worth a life.

You are worth your ☼life and your presence
on others.

Chocolate

September 26, 2018

You want her to melt in those hands,

So, you can devour her.

You want her to be sweet,

Yet she has a side of spice never
bitterness.

You want to be able to mold her,

And create a woman you will value.

You want a Hersey's kiss,

a kiss filled with her sugary love.

Or do you want a love that's bliss?

A love that will never be left in your
pocket to melt.

Early Mornings

September 28, 2018

Every morning I set my alarm 10 minutes
early

Just to cuddle with you for 5 minutes

And try to wake you up for 5 more.

You're hard to wake up when you snore.

Every morning I rub your waves until you
awake

I say a prayer for you to go about your day

And I send positive vibes your way

Like I can protect you from your enemies.

Every morning I kiss you on your forehead

If you're lucky, you'll get a kiss on your
cheek

Just so I can see you smile

Then go to the bathroom to pee.

Every morning, I watch your body move

In broken pieces from the hard day before.

I see your body in pain

Yet I see you put one foot into your
uniform pants

Every morning, I notice how you stand
around

Like a kid getting ready for school

Just to convince yourself it's 3 am

And you have to go to work to impress them.

Every morning, you give me hugs and plead

To stay under this warm blanket with me

And hug me and give me morning kisses

Morning kisses...

Every morning, I walk downstairs

In my t shirt, panties, and a blanket

Sharing my love for you

And preparing you mentally for a good day.

Every morning I debate on whether or not

To sleep on your pillow after you leave

I know it's covered in your slob

But waking up to you makes my heart throb.

Smile

October 8, 2018

Seeing your smile adds to mine

Your smile is a sight to see

I want to be able to make you happy

Every single day naturally

Happier than you were yesterday

or the day before that

I want to make you happier

every single chance that I get

Live in the now and not wonder how

you will make it to tomorrow

Sit back and relax

just to get rid of all of your sorrow.

enjoy the sunshine

and the rain

enjoy the good times

and learn from the pain

Enjoy this moment

it is worth your while

but baby

Your smile will never go out of style.

Security

October 10,2018

Can I consider you a shield
from all things evil
or should I shield myself from you?

They say only the people
you love can hurt you,
well I love you.

They say if something is meant to be
then it will always comeback.
don't leave.

They say we're too young
to know anything about love,
well I want to learn.

I want to live in the present
the past cannot hold me back
from the future I see in you.

I want to unlock my heart
without the fear of heartbreak.
Don't break. Don't crack.

Letter to my younger self

October 13, 2018

Dear 12-year-old me,

        You will get over this divorce. Your parents still love you the same. You will have a tough time transitioning from Mississippi with your parents to Columbus, Georgia with your mom, but you will manage. School will be different as far as culture, but you will fit right in. Don't worry. You will eventually be living with your older sister who is very jealous of you, but don't let that affect your behavior or confidence. Even though she will blackmail you by using your father as a rope. Your father will make you cry a lot with his military, uniformed love that may be too tough for such a young girl, but don't forget that he loves you. Your mother may not always be able to provide for you with named brands and the latest phone, but she is trying. Going from a marriage to a single parent isn't easy. Be nicer to her when you don't always get what you want for your birthday or Christmas.

        One day, you will wake up and hear her praying for you and crying in the bathroom because she if afraid that she is losing you to depression and rebellion. You will pretend you are still sleeping, but maybe you should give her a hug and tell her you love and appreciate her. Try not to cry too much, you will understand when you get my age that you could have used that energy somewhere else.

Friends are nonexistent after high school. They will all disappear. LOL Anyways, dating is a thing girl. Don't let it scare you. The boy you meet freshman year, of high school will really like you, but don't date him as a favor... You were never interested in him. Spare his heart. Oh, that guy from high school, the basketball player you will meet junior year, he will not be the love of your life, but he will teach you a few lessons that you will need to know. 1. Never love someone more than they love you. 2. Don't mark up your skin to show your pain. 3. Your poetry is your weapon. USE IT! (Now I am currently crying)

Depression and anxiety will kill you, only if you let it. Don't let it. Pick you a pen and write. Now let's talk about college because you are going. Your dad's GI Bill covers it, so you get to go to college for free. This is not a freebee. College is not a game. You will be in the magnet program and National Honor Society. You will feel super smart, but college will tear your confidence down. Do not procrastinate. Be sure to study. Always communicate with your instructors. Sophomore year of college, you would have gone through way too many heart breaks to handle. This will make you venerable. A female you work with will approach you, she likes you and wants to hang out. Don't do it. She will give you the best memories of your life, fall in love with you and ruin your future all at the same time. Then she will propose, you will say yes, but that is not

what you actually want. You simply want to be unconditionally loved.

You do not have to rush your life honey. Be patient and the right one will come to you. Speaking of the right one, he could possibly pop up at the end of your relationship to catch you as you fall. As of right now, I will say let him. I will write you again to see if he was a love or a lesson. He wants to meet your dad, so it has to be serious right... Nobody's met your well our dad before. Scary feeling. I guess he actually wants to get to know you. Once you meet him, your baby fever will top the charts. Try to get rid of it for your sanity. Again, do not rush your life because you fear you will die before completing everything on your list. Be patient. Be kind. This letter is way longer than expected. I have an appointment with my psychologist on Wednesday at 9:15 am. I am going to read her this letter. Keep your head up girl.

LOOOOOVE,

19-year-old Cierra

who turns 20 on October 20th.

Happy early birthday girl!!!

Psych Eval.

October 17, 2018

Are you in any pain?
No unless we are talking mentally.
Have you thought about suicide in the past
year?
Yes, but I at least think of self-harm
during the course of a really bad day.
Have you thought about harming or killing
someone else?
No. I don't think I've reached that level
of crazy.
On a scale of 1-10, how would you rate your
day?
Why isn't there a negative on this scale, I
am barely alive here?
Are you having trouble sleeping or staying
asleep?
Yes, sleeping becomes a nightmare before I
can even close my eyes.
On a scale from strongly disagree to
strongly agree, rate this statement. I have
trouble maintaining relationships with my
friends, family, or significant other.
Strongly agree, I push everyone away from
me. I am a ticking time bomb. 3, 2, wait.
On a scale from 1-10, how would you rate
your anxiety?
20 like my heart is beating out of my

chest. Do you see it? I cannot breathe.
How often do you feel depressed?
Everyday. I can start off good but by the
end of the day my bed is calling me in for
my daily coma appointment.

What makes you happy?
I am not sure that's why I am here seeking
your services. I expect you to have the
answer.
On a scale of 1-10, rate your mood swings.
10 meaning I constantly swing from high to
low. I am a rollercoaster.
Are you on medicine?
I was on escitalopram for two months until
they decided not to refill my prescription.
I went cold turkey by default and had a
nervous breakdown. I went to the emergency
room. It was either there or hell.
Now can you fix me?

Unborn Child

November 7, 2018

In the beginning,

God created the heavens and the earth.

In the midst of it all,

he will bless me with you.

You will be showered with love and
positivity.

You will be the greatest gift God could
give this earth

and a blessing that only could be sent by
the heavens.

There will be peace all around you.

Natural waterbirth with rose petals,
lilies, and carnations.

Rhythm and blues will play in the
background until you arrive.

Candles will be lit all around, but they
will not outshine you.

I cannot wait until you're no longer a
pigment of my imagination.

Living Room Floor

December 6, 2018

I scroll through Netflix with the PS4
controller

in one hand and the Brunswick

burger you made in the other.

Bone and Blood is what you suggested we
watch.

Wait.

Maybe it was titled Blood and Bone.

Anyways,

we snuggle together under the faux fur
blanket

and eat our burgers and nacho cheese
Doritos.

The movie plays, and one scene made me want
to be spontaneous.

So, I did exactly that.

I don't mind goofing off, if it made you
smile.

I wanted to reenact the push-pull scene.

I doubt it was called that, but that's what
I will call it.

You and I swaying in the middle of the
living room floor.

It was a weird movement,

but with you I wanted to try it anyways.

No one was watching us.

Swaying turned into slow dancing.

Randomly slow dancing on the living room
floor.

There was no music to hear, we didn't need
any for a moment like this.

You say, "Follow my lead. I will show you
what my grandma taught me."

I will follow wherever you go.

I step where you step.

Move when you tell me to.

Spin when you lift your hand up.

We became one on my living room floor.

I am so grateful for your grandma.

She showed you how to slow dance,

so, you then showed me.

This moment will forever be

in my memory

even when old age hits.

Thank you.

Abortion

December 9, 2018

I'm against abortion,
But my mother isn't.
What if she aborted me
And I became nonexistent?

What if the entire world changed
Just because I was not born.
What if? What if I was not here?
There would be one less headache.

I mean I know I am a hell raiser
Bringing what's below to the human view,
But I'm sure my sins are not as big as you.
I'm sure aborting me, would of been a big
mistake.

I know I gave you more grey hairs on your
head
And I'm sure I've caused you a lot of
money,
But what if one day, just one
I came back to haunt you screaming mommy.

And the child that survived your guilt
after me
Wasn't healthy, did someone say karma?

What if this was viewed as murder?
Abortion: n. The act of killing what will
be known to become a human...

With fingernails.

Babies have fingernails!
I have a swinging tale
To tell my kids before they set sail.

Your grandma said that if we were not
prepared for you
We should get rid of you
But I disagree.
Everything will be fine even if it's just
you and me.

Glass

December 9, 2018

Clear

Shattering

Pieces of purity

Breaking

At the touch of her strength

At the beats of her heart

At the moment when

No one labeled the package as fragile

I'm guessing

They wanted her

To break.

Perfect

December 9, 2018

When things are going too well
Something is wrong.
It's there but no one pays attention.
The problem is right in front of you
Between you and him.
The issue that makes you two
anything but perfect.

Imagine

December 9, 2018

Marriage

Kids

Nice house

With a white picket fence

Nice car

Great career

All

Are

A

Pigment

Of

My

Imagination

Her

December 10, 2018

She means nothing to you.

Well that's not the point.

What do I mean to you?

That's a hard point to prove.

You see if she was nothing

you wouldn't risk something

or even your everything

to be with nothing.

Why gamble the lottery away

to pick up a penny off of the sidewalk?

Why throw away a queen

to lay up with a peasant?

I give you everything.

More than I gave the last.

More than I have to give.

More than I get in return.

I am not her.

I am Cierra.

Who is worth more than her.

She's a nameless entity.

A nobody.

Yet she could have caused you

the best thing that has happened to you.

A nobody should never compete with your
everything.

Remember that

Next time you let a nobody

draw you away from who matters the most.

Shame on you.

Shame on me.

Reflect

December 10, 2018

Look in the mirror.

Can you even recognize your reflection?

Can you see the pain in your eyes?
...the burdens on your shoulders?
...the guilt all over your face?

Can you see it?
...the happiness you're faking?
...the hearts you are breaking?
...and the bullshit you are creating?

Can you see a way out?
...the beginning of the cycle?
...the end of the pain?
...the need for a change?

Close your eyes.

Do you see me now?

Hate

December 10, 2018

I was always told that hate is a strong
word.

I agree.

It is a strong feeling of hurt, betrayal,
pain,

trials and tribulations, nights of crying,
nights of praying,

fights, more crying, doubt, lack of trust,
lack of stability,

lack of everything, lack of support, lack
of feeling,

I hate all of these things.

Who am I?

December 17, 2018

I must admit that I have lost myself

along the way of self-discovery

I forgot what I was meant to be

I cannot recognize the reflection I see.

I used to be filled with spontaneity,

adventure, and living life on the edge

Where did that girl go?

I'm asking myself, and I still do not know.

Renege

December 19, 2018

Friends?

Is that really all you want to be?

I love our vibe and our chemistry.

I want you to know what you mean to me.

I wanted more than just sexual relations,

dinner and a movie, fun without
limitations,

long car talks to past the time,

the closer we got, the more I wanted you to
be mine.

Our pace was abnormal

but I wouldn't complain

except for right now

when we don't feel the same.

You're a contradiction.

Torn between your heart and your mind,

confused by your past and current time.

You do not know what you want. I do not
know what to give.

I mean, that is okay...

except for when you said "I love you"
first.

And when you wanted to meet my father

before giving me the title as your
girlfriend,

or when you bought me a puppy

just to see me smile,

or when you considered sex

not your average fuck, but love being made,

or when you proposed the idea of marriage

without an actual proposal,

or when you decided we should start looking
for apartments and engagement rings.

These are all of the reasons why I love
you.

You love me, but you just aren't sure what
to do.

One incident was not one to many.

It should not interfere with our happy
ending.

Why take a step back to the basics?

You are my oasis

when I am hit with poker faces

avoiding those dark, haunted, forbidden
places.

I said, "Are you sure you want me, I have a
lot of baggage?"

You said, "Of course girl, let me help you
carry all of that baggage."

You had me then, in the palm of your hands.

Especially, when you thought you lost me
for you kneeled beside my bed and prayed.

Now I have the pear shape with a single
halo engagement ring stuck in my head

along with the two-bedroom apartment at The
Lakes we both fell in love with.

And we can't forget about how we told
selected love ones about our 2019 plans

and now that you've reneged, their
questions hurt.

Your dad said "I love you and Cici, and I
know you love her.

I support the marriage. I know that you
want to marry her,

so, what's the problem?"

The problem is you just aren't ready for
all of the things you told me to be ready
for in 2019.

Just know that I love you

and time spent with you is not regretted or
wasted,

but I hope that one day

you won't doubt my ability to be your wife

and your ability to be my husband.

Love,

Red Heart

Anything

December 27, 2018

Don't you hate

the feeling of confusion?

Where your mind

is trying to put together

Pieces of a puzzle

that are not even meant to be

the same picture?

Or when you're trying

to read someone's mind because their
actions and words never seem to add up?

Or when you're alone and you cry

Because you just don't know anything?

Dear Future Husband,

December 27, 2018

I know you're not ready,
But when you are ready
My dear future husband
I will be ready to
Love you without conditions,
Obstacles, or doubt
Wake up to you every day
With you staring back at me
With those gleaming brown eyes
Push you towards your goals,
Future plans and aspirations
Support your dreams
Even if everyone else doesn't believe in
you
Ask you about your day and never put my
happy days over your bad ones
Make you smile and laugh
About how corny your wife can be, oh yea
That's going to be me
Pray for you day in and day out
Until God can hear my thoughts and whispers
Wash your back
Even when you're willing and able
Feed you with not only meals
But with the words to let you know

how much you are valued and loved
Nurture you without replacing your mom

Just helping her son stay healthy mentally
and physically, and of course spiritually.

Making sure I keep our marriage
Spicy and I promise to never be boring
I promise to be a worthy wife
I promise to be an amazing mother
And most of all I promise to say I do when
you finally decided that I am the only
woman you need.
I know you can't do that right now,
But I will wait for you to be the man
You need to be to fully invest in me
Once you've fully invested into yourself.
I will wait for my Prince Charming to come
I just hope he hears my call.

You

December 27, 2018

You are my happiness.

Please don't run away from me.

Match

December 27, 2018

Loving someone

More

Than they will allow

Themselves to love you

Is the hardest pill

To swallow.

Your love for them

Will always be greater

Because you're not afraid to love

Let alone be loved.

See no Evil

December 27, 2018

You couldn't look me

In the eyes

Knowing that all

You would see

Is the broken part of me

Where I questioned

Your actions and words

I began to doubt your

Love for me

I lost all trust in you

Nothing left but

A reflection of my crying eyes

In the center of your lying eyes

You captured my pain

The pain you have caused.

After all of the destruction

And pain, you couldn't get enough

You begged me to do what weakens me

Looking into your eyes
I saw past your past

To see the devil himself
Staring back at me

Summer in January

December 31,2018

I have always thought of you as a daughter,

Even though you had a mommy and daddy of
your own,

But this time, something was different.

You stole my heart all over again.

You are so beautiful.

You just need proper loving

To fully develop into the young lady

I would want you to be

To separate you from this society.

Your mom should be ashamed of herself.

Anyone should be considered lucky to be
your mom.

You did not ask to be here,

Yet I am glad you are here with me.

I thought that this was going to be a play
date

With the little cousin that I adore,

But instead I can now see the world

Through her tiny, virgin eyes.

Picture a five-year-old saying…

"Your home is my home now."

"I want to live with you forever."

"Good morning mommy, I love you."

Imagine hearing a pure child say…

"I have to protect you from the darkness."

"You don't need anyone, but me."

"I don't want to go back home."

Now vividly visualize

Summer: "Can I do to work with you?"

Me: "No baby you cannot."

Summer: "Why do you have to work?"

Me: "Well, I have to get paid to take you
to Chuckie Cheese."

Summer: "I don't want to go if you have to
leave me."

How could your heart not melt?

How could you neglect such an angel?

How could she not motivate you

to do better?

Could she at least get the life she is
choosing?

Could she at least feel loved at all times?

No air

January 4, 2019

December 19, I took you to the airport

To fly to Tyler, Texas.

You would not be returning until January 6,
2019

To Fort Benning to return to reality.

17 days.

I was scared.

You did not leave on the best of terms

I was very insecure because my trust for
you was gone.

I was not enough for you, but she was.

My heart could not take losing you,

Even though I would consider myself a prize
too.

You wanted something more.

I was not enough for you.

It was as simple as someone giving you
sexual attention.

Someone to talk dirty to you.

Someone to talk a good game.
My lack of experience put me on the bench.

I just want to get in the game.
Maybe I need more practice and training,
But don't count me out coach.
Don't bring in someone from the side lines.

Chapter 3

She is…

Lost & found

Escitalopram

I shed tears from time to time randomly.

As I fall down to the floor, I am
screaming,

And crying and screaming while dying.

Grabbing a blade gives me power

To do what I want to do with my body.

Cover it in blood-filled cuts

That eventually turn into scars in a hidden
cry for help.

I engraved H-E-L-P once and broke down
after the P

And just before the Escitalopram.

The Feels

January 22,2019

The moon lights up the night sky

the same way this candle

is lighting up the room.

When there is darkness

there will be light soon.

The lingering amber scent,

sent my adrenaline to a rush.

Intense intimacy

galore of chemistry

Hand and hand

chest to chest

We became one.

Power

January 16,2019

The day I realized that

I had the power

to move mountains

was the day I realized

that I must never doubt my abilities.

The day I picked up a pen and a journal

instead of a blade and my thigh

was the day I realized

I had power over my depression.

The day I made a man cry

at the thought of losing me

was the day I realized

I am worth more than

what others value me.

And the day I

stood up for something I believed in

was the day I realized

that power is all in the mind.

A weak mind

will never have power.

But a strong mind

can create enough power

to turn a sinner into a saint.

Pushy

January 24,2018

I'm sorry for being so pushy
But I see a future with you
And that's not something I say
To someone I've known so briefly

I was nervous at first
About you and I
That's what took me so long
To even reply

But once I knew that
I wanted to be more than friends
I could not let
This feeling end

I took it upon myself
To present my love
Like a proposal
Except all I had to offer was my love

I decided that I had to be your girl
It was a necessity
And that was just in the beginning
Now I feel like I am rushing
And my time is ending

I have dreamed for a prince like you
To remind me that dreams do come true
You're my fairytale and my fantasy
You're my dream and I don't want to wake up

You motivate me
Inspire me
And keep me grounded and humble
my dear guardian angel

You've rescued me from a dark place
And my love for you is internal and
external
*I am crying while typing this

I love you more than
Saying I love you.
More than words can express
If you don't see it by now,
then baby I can't tell you the rest.

Hidden Treasure

January 25,2019

If I could share my love for you
with the world,
Then I would scream at the top
of the highest mountain

"I love...You"
You know who you are.
But
If you could share your love
For me at a restaurant
Would you even have the courage

To stand up on the table
And cause a scene
just to say " I love her"
You know what you will do.
But
If I am yours and you are mine,
Then what's wrong with the world knowing?
What's wrong with people seeing our
happiness?
What's the big deal about keeping us hidden
away socially?
Am I not enough?
I know I am more than enough.
Wait, I wonder if these girls that don't
know about us capture you with their
temptation?
I wonder if they even ask about me?
You can't ask about what you don't know,

right?
Can't talk about what's left in the
shadows.

Why do you leave me in the darkness when I
am as yellow as a star shining bright?

PSA

January 29, 2019

Stop telling women
that they are enough
or even more than enough!
Your actions will then show her
that she was...
a little bit too much
for you to deal with.
Too high strong
Too worthy of more
Too sensitive
Too bull headed
Because she may be all of those things,
But one thing she is not...
WEAK.

Weakened by the words
You whisper
Or yell
Into her innocent ears
Of all the dark secrets you will tell
Her.
Her as in your girl, your queen,
Your rider, your friend
Your dream girl.
Maybe that is not enough for you.
She wants to be your everything.
Your lover, your best friend, your doctor,
Your homeboy, your therapist, your
challenger, but never your enemy.
She just wants to be yours
And only yours.

Stop making her feel as if
you need more
From everyone else below her.
Why can't your queen
Handle all of these things on her own?
She handles your bullshit,
Your excuses,
Your cries,
And your apologies,
Why can't she handle
Your smile,
Laughs,
Good times,
Love?

Don't dish out the bad and save the good
for everyone else.

She can handle it all.

Now give it to her.

Silent Cries

January 30, 2019

The sun is shining into her eyes
Yet she is crying silently
The moon finds her crying eyes
And tries to put her to sleep soundly

She pays attention to her breathing
In...Out...
Her chest tightens
As if she lacks oxygen

She hears a voice
In her head saying
Do not cry in front of this foe
He will see that you are weak

So she continues to hold her head down
And continues to cry
Waiting just waiting
For someone to ask her why

She's silently crying
At the thought of this happiness
Only being temporarily here
But what about forever?

What good are you for me temporarily
When you will just hurt me permanently?
Permanently scarred
From a temporary source of joy.

Wake up

January 30,2019

I look at you as if you are

the perfect image of what I want.

Are you?

Well,

You are who I want to mature with

...have fun with,

...and struggle with.

You are the person that I have prayed for

...longed for

... and waited for.

You are the one I would cry to

... fly to

.... and open up my heart to.

I mean.

I would give my last for you.

I would be there if you lost it all.

I would motivate you

when everyone is knocking you down after
your fall.

5 Hours

January 30,2019

We had an argument the night before.

It lasted damn near 2 days on and off.

I slept with this on my brain for 5 hours
on and off.

I tossed, and I turned.

Trying to figure out how this would turn
out.

Make up or break up?

Put up a fight or surrender.

7:00 PM and you're in the passenger seat
upset.

Shouldn't I be the one upset?

You're mine, you're taken, you're happy,
right?

Well why do you still have a tinder?

30 minutes go by.

Silence fills my car like me sleeping while
in the state of depression.

Words are spoken.

Short and unsweetened.

Please tell me what is on your mind.

How do we go from potentially perfect to
one big imperfection?

Moral of the story is

I am lost and losing feeling towards things
I cannot control.

I love you and you love me,

but that will never be enough in this
society.

"You are everything I prayed for," you
said.

"You are who I want and need," I replied.

But that is not enough for you.

You are afraid.

That we are being stupid on our early 20s.

That we are only temporarily happy and
content.

We cannot get married now.

We will fuck up.

He said, "I am not ready."

I said, "No you just don't understand the
bigger picture."

If we are dating, then we will make
mistakes.

If we are newly married, we will mess up.

If we have been married for 20 years,

then we may consider a divorce.

If we have a child,

Then we may want to raise them differently.

If you wanted to make a change in your
career,

then I will be there to motivate you.

If hell is where we are briefly,
then we will find our way back to earth.

5 hours of this car talk later
and I just have one question.

The question is...

am I the person you want to go through

hell, to get to heaven with?

Shea and Cocoa

February 8,2019

Push down and twist

the top off the baby oil

Turn the lights off

and let the string lights string me along.

Silence.

I lie on the bed

bare and pure

natural and fragile.

You pour the baby oil

all over my covered spine to ease my mind

filled with stress and weary.

No time to pour it into the palm of your
hands,

which is exactly where you had me.

condensed bottle to a tingling body
tingling body to itching hand
itching hand to yellow under-toned skin
that relaxes at your touch.

You caress my skin.
Neck to shoulders,
shoulders to back
back to my panties
pulling them down my legs
fingering my juices that flow.

And boy do they flow for you.
Like how you bite a juicy apple
and the juice slips off your lips.
Oh, how slippery I am when wet

take caution.

We trade places
I sit on you to drizzle oil on your back
and unplug the stringed lights

just so that the moon can see this.

A massage given, received, and reciprocated

built up too much chemistry to resist.

My lady box throbbing like a heartbeat to
feel you.

I needed to feel all of your loving.

I ask for a goodnight kiss

but we didn't go to sleep.

When the kissing became too intense

I whispered, "please don't leave me"

holding back tears because I am so in love
with you.

You replied, "I could never."

I believed you.

The next day

we questioned if that was the first time we
made love.

We didn't fuck. We didn't just have sex.

This was different.

About Me

February 8,2019

I've had songs written about me
Tears shed over me
Lives chanced because of me
Yet I'm sitting here reading my poetry

I've been human
I've been a zombie
I've been a ghost
But no blade against me can prosper.

I've had people spend their last on me
People who didn't want to spend a damn dime
And people who intentionally wasted my time
Fuck you.

I've had my toes kissed
While working their lips up to my lips
You decide which ones they got to first.

I've had people
who were not good enough
To even be in my existence

And yes I am that good
Yes they are that unworthy
I am a queen.

I am worth something
Yet you cannot buy me

I've had people treat me exactly how I
hoped to be treated
Yet I still left them
Something was missing.

I've had people get signs from God, the
universe, family and friends
Yet they were still not sure I was the one
for them.

Who am I the one for?
I don't want to be a rebound
Don't want second place
I want to be on top.

I want to be the only one
You need and want.
I'm neither to you
But to myself I am everything.

Plentiful

February 8,2019

I've had an abundance of lovers
Or should I say fuckers
Who didn't mean me any good
Any.

They loved me but
They also loved many.
Way too many.

I would give to them my all
But apparently I didn't give them plenty.

When they needed to make a dollar
And they only had 99 cents
I was their pretty penny.

I'm worth way more
Than your bullshit.

3 words

I appreciate you.

I want you.

I love you.

I need you.

I adore you.

I trust you.

I believe you.

I forgive you.

I see you.

I feel you.

I hear you.

I taste you.

I smell you.

Say three words

and you can

change the way

you make her

feel about you.

At first

I am scrolling through my phone as I am
typing this.

I go all the way back to August 2018,

which was when we first met.

I am not a cool kid, so my kickback failed.

We ended up downtown trying to find a move

My best friend decided to be bold and send
you a message,

Hey, we are downtown, so you should pull
up?

To seal the deal...

She sent my location.

You came.

Driving 25 minutes away from the barracks
to see me.

A strange girl, who

matched with you on Tinder,

who would play with your emotions
accidentally

by saying hi

and leaving it at goodbye

and then saying hello,

just to say that I have to go.

I was in awe of you baby.

Nervousness filled my stomach so much

that I am sure you felt like I was avoiding
you.

I was avoiding the fact that staring into
your eyes

could make me fall in love.

What is love at first sight,

when it is not a shared connection?

2 months

We had sex.

It was not good.

I was inexperienced,

but the juices would still flow good.

I lacked chemistry with you.

Sex was a thing I expected to do.

Sex in this generation was a need in a
relationship.

We were not in a relationship yet,

but I wanted to be more than friends.

I haven't had sex with the opposite sex

in more than the different ways a
translator can say sex.

I was not able to take what Texas gave you.

I was not a hit it and quit it like what
the game told you.

I needed more and so did you.

I had a lot of baggage and you did too.

You could have left me then,
but somehow you managed
I am not sure if it was my mind
that gave me such an advantage.

The more we talked
the better our relationship grew.
The more we talked
the better sex was with you.

You had to get into me mentally
before I can physically catch up.
Now we are having sex too often
and I cannot catch up.

Sex before marriage is a sin
but sex before a relationship is worse.
You will be giving yourself to a man
like giving away all of the money in your
purse.

I noticed my value.

I figured out the key.

In order for me to get the respect I needed

It has to be you and me.

So, sex happened on my bed.

Sex broke my bed.

Sex broke me mentally.

I asked a question to determine

Whether this would be the end of me.

Are you going to ask me out or what?

We cannot keep doing this without meaning
behind a title.

I demanded what I wanted and got it.

I am sorry if my values made you feel as if
you were being held hostage.

-a woman who gives and wanted to receive

3 Hours

X on your heart

Your heart became my target

I shot a couple of times

But I am not Cupid

I guess I needed some practice

I guess I needed to reroute this

Location pending

Destination never ending

Feel Me

I wish you would feel me
As I am restless at night
Tossing until my heart
Turns in my chest,

Lying next you
In this bed
On the other side
Unreachable

Unbearable
This feeling is
Like a bear I must
Hibernate

Hiding away from my mind
Earth and it's evil

I don't want to hide from you
I want you to open up
Like a wound that's been cut too deep
You will need stitches

I will examine you
Love you
Stitch you
And fix you

But first you need to feel me

Lying next to you in this bed
Restless at night
As my opinion has its biggest bite

Zzz

Snore
For,
and, nor,
but, or,
yet, so
Just like these conjunctions
I hear you snore throughout the night
Adding to the fan that blows
And my stomach that's growling
as the voice in my head that's reading this
As I type it continues to override it all.
My conscience has fled a couple of times
Especially with a blade doing what they do
best cutting down eyebrows,
Wow I can't even think of self-harm anymore
A better line should of been
-best cutting through the skin I have
sinned
Or
-best cutting through the scars I left from
the last time
Or
-best cutting the bullshit...
I like the last one better,
Less intense
More of a be free feel
I seemed to have healed
I am not sure why exactly
But my brain thinks differently

It's tainted just not poisoned
It's toxic just not fatal
I am okay with that
I just wish you were awake right now
Because my mind is on a race track
And baby I cannot sleep.

Gone

I woke up and you were gone.
Good thing it was a dream,
Right?

Stiff.

Numb.

Invisible.

Bed

I make my bed up and lie in it
Even when I'm in it
I'm still
I can't move the covers
And make room for monsters.

I used to

Cut myself

As a punishment

For loving

You

I cried in front of you.

You did not even notice.

-invisibility is not a gift

Update

February 11, 2019

I am no longer suicidal.

I have not cut myself in over a year.

I am handling my depression and anxiety on
my own.

I am no longer or Lexapro or Zoloft.

I have an emotional rescue pup named Faith.

I am in a happy relationship.

By the time I write my next book,

I should she be married to my military
husband,

Pregnant or with my first born,

Living in the suburbs, and

Teaching at an elementary school.

Those poems should be filled with a lot
more joy.

My life will be completed with all things
good.

I am content with my life and I am excited
about my future.

Message to all:

Do not let a series of unfortunate events be what defines you.

Your life is valued.

You are not a waste of space.

If anyone belittles you, then come to me directly.

I am here for people who have no one.

I am here for people who has everyone surrounding them, yet they still feel alone.

I am here for you.

You are awesome.

Like you are really fucking awesome.

I love you, you are awesome strangers, who are no longer strangers once you read my book.

Keep being a solider, unicorn, warrior, zebra, whatever makes you comfortable and feel strong. Keep on doing what you do!